for Emma and Faustine

minedition

North American edition published 2020 by minedition, New York

Text and illustrations copyright © 2020 Sylvie Auzary-Luton
Coproduction with Michael Neugebauer Publishing Ltd., Hong Kong.
Rights arranged with "minedition ag", Zurich, Switzerland. All rights reserved.
Michael Neugebauer Publishing Ltd.,
19 West 21st Street, #1201, New York, NY 10010
e-mail: info@minedition.com
This book was printed in May 2020 at Hong Kong Discovery Printing Company Limited.
3/F., Blue Box Factory Building, 25 Hing Wo Street, Tin Wan, Aberdeen, Hong Kong, China
Typesetting in Corbel
Library of Congress Cataloging-in-Publication Data available upon request.

ISBN 978-1-6626-5004-8
10 9 8 7 6 5 4 3 2 1
First Impression

For more information please visit our website: www.minedition.com

Eugene
and the sounds of the city

Sylvie Auzary-Luton

minedition

Eugene loves to dance.

He dances all the time,
anywhere, to any noise.

clic

cloc

cloc

clic

clic

clic

Eugene can hear the rhythm in any sound. He grabs hold of it, repeats the tempo, and invents a new dance step to go along with it. He'll dance to anything.

SKITCH-SKATCH CLOCKODOC PomPom TIK

Eugene dreams of dancing with everyone he sees. He wants to share his joy.

IKIDI *PEOOT-PEOOT* **BOombam** TIC-TIC **GLOG-GLOG** pitili

But the busy city folks aren't interested.

Eugene doesn't mind. He smiles from ear to ear as he bops down the boulevard.

He rhumbas to the rumble of buses, he pirouettes to the beeping scooters.
But the hurried bystanders don't take much notice of him.

Eugene bounces with the jackhammer...

Wheeee waaah

...and salsas with the sirens of fire engines,
while the bustling crowd remains indifferent.

Wheeee waaah

Eugene capers with the construction machines and boogies to the bicycle bells, but the drivers just give him funny looks.

"Such noise, it's music to my ears!"
Eugene thinks.

The hurried passers-by stop and stare at Eugene.
"Come, dance with me!" he exclaims. But no one else hears the tempo.

When a car horn concert begins, Eugene throws himself into the noise.
He whirls and jumps and twirls like he never has before.
The pace is racing. "This is magic!" he thinks to himself.

Suddenly Eugene stops. Everyone is yelling at him.

"Stop blocking traffic!"

"Why are you jumping around?"

"Get out of the way!"

Eugene is taken aback. He tries to explain the rhythm
of the jackhammer, the tempo of the horns…

But nobody wants to hear it.
Everyone is angry.
Eugene trudges away from
the traffic jam, dejected.

Eugene walks back slowly through the narrow side streets,
avoiding the crowds. In the silence he can hear his own footsteps,
growing quieter and quieter.

He realizes there's snow falling around him,
covering the city's noises in a blanket of stillness.
Eugene listens hard, and he can hear the faint
puff of soft flakes piling up around him.

Now Eugene has a new idea.
He starts to move slowly and smoothly.

He sways gently to this peaceful new rhythm,
and he starts to feel his heart lift up.

crunch

crunch

crunch

Soon others join him, feeling the same rhythm. Then even more come along, and Eugene can hear their dancing feet crunching in the snow.

At last, together, in the silence of a winter evening, they reinvent the noises of the city.

BANG

boom boom boom

crunch crunch

piing

click clock

Before long the crowd is exploding with rhythm and laughter, and everyone dances together, just as Eugene had always dreamed.